Piggies

Dedicated to Marjane Wood

www.HarcourtBooks.com

The Library of Congress has cataloged an earlier edition as follows:
Wood, Don, 1945–
Piggies/Don and Audrey Wood; illustrated by Don Wood.
p.   cm.
Summary: Ten little piggies dance on a young child's fingers and toes before finally going to sleep.
[1. Bedtime—Fiction.   2. Games—Fiction.   3. Pigs—Fiction.]
I. Wood, Audrey.   II. Title.
PZ7.W84737P1   1991
[E]—dc20   89-24598
ISBN-13: 978-0-15-256341-7 hc   ISBN-10: 0-15-256341-5 hc
ISBN-13: 978-0-15-205667-4 book and CD   ISBN-10: 0-15-205667-X book and CD

First Harcourt book-and-musical-CD edition 2006

C E G H F D B

The paintings in this book were done in oil on Bristol board.
The display type was set in Caxton Book.
The text type was set in Goudy Catalog.
Composition by Thompson Type, San Diego, California
Color separations by Bright Arts, Ltd., Singapore
Printed and bound by Tien Wah Press, Singapore
This book was printed on totally chlorine-free Stora Enso Matte paper.
Production supervision by Ginger Boyer
Designed by Michael Farmer

Printed in Singapore

Piggies

WRITTEN BY

DON AND AUDREY WOOD

ILLUSTRATED BY

DON WOOD

Harcourt, Inc.

Orlando Austin New York San Diego Toronto London

I've got two

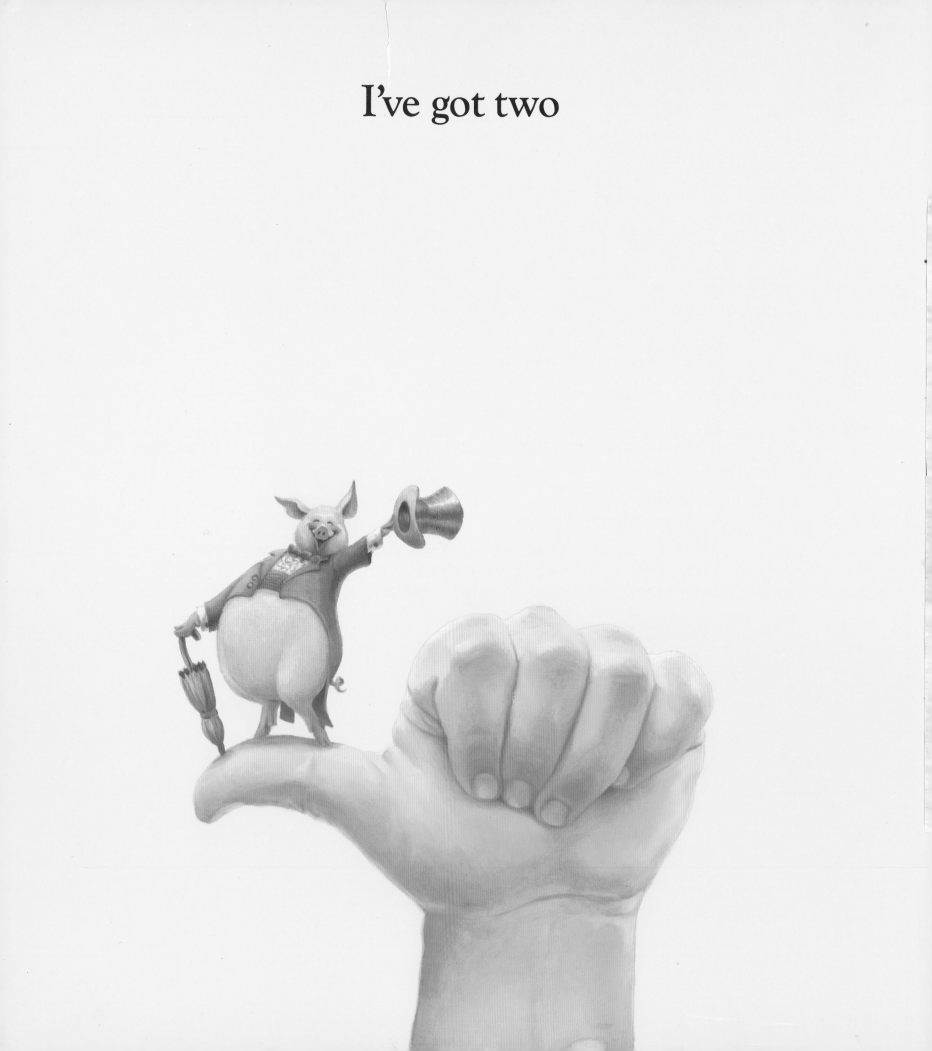

fat little piggies,

two smart

little piggies,

two   long

little piggies,

two silly

little piggies,

and two wee

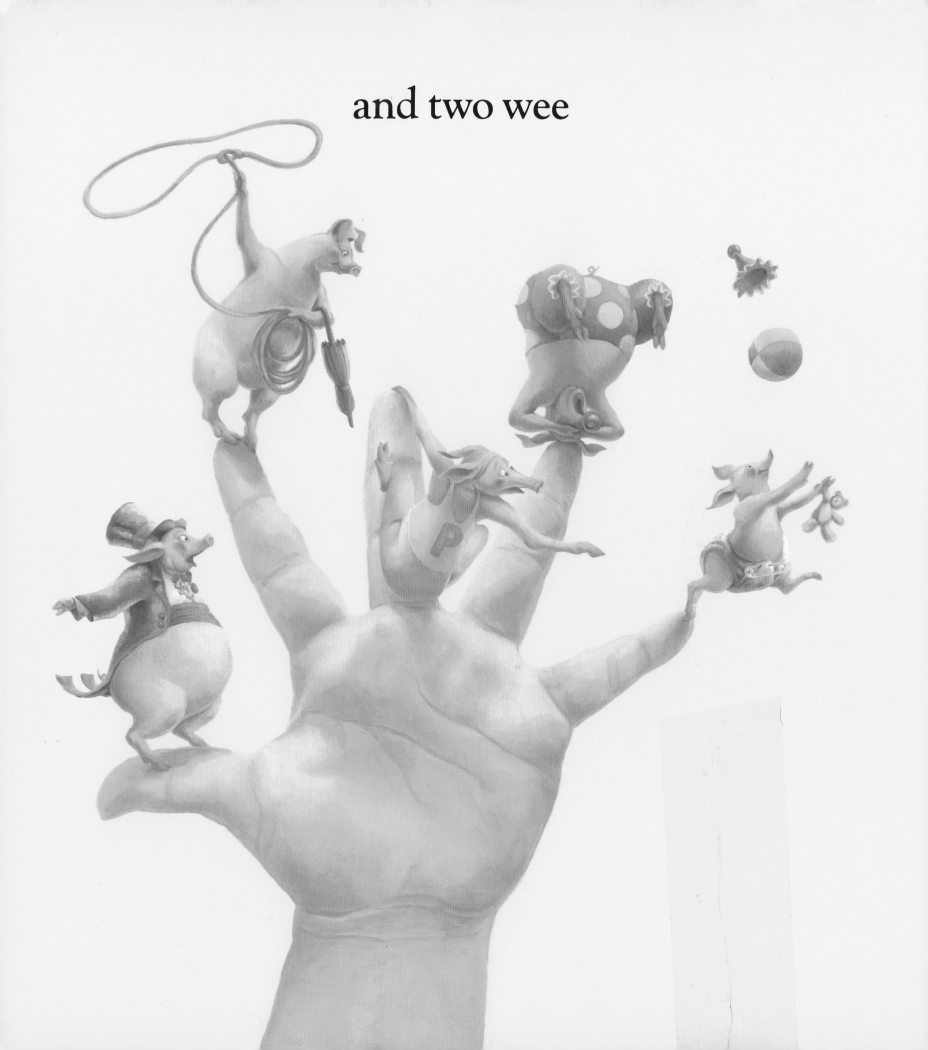

little piggies.

Sometimes they're

hot little piggies,

and sometimes they're

cold little piggies.

Sometimes they're

clean little piggies,

and sometimes they're

dirty little piggies.

Sometimes they're

good little piggies,

but not at bedtime. That's when

they skip down my tummy,

dance on my toes,

then run away and hide.

So . . .

. . . I put them together, all in a row,
for two fat kisses,
two smart kisses,
two long kisses,
two silly kisses,

and two wee kisses goodnight.